# MYTHS AND LEGENDS OF AOTEAROA

RETOLD BY

## ANNIE RAE TE AKE AKE

ILLUSTRATED BY

## NEW ZEALAND SECONDARY SCHOOL ARTISTS

SCHOLASTIC

AUCKLAND    SYDNEY    NEW YORK    LONDON    TORONTO
MEXICO CITY    NEW DELHI    HONG KONG

*I dedicate this book to my beloved mokopuna,*
*Daniel, Benji, Valeska and Danielle*

Published by Scholastic New Zealand Limited, 1999
Private Bag 94407, Greenmount, Auckland 1730, New Zealand.

Scholastic Australia Pty Limited
PO Box 579, Gosford, NSW 2250, Australia.

Scholastic Inc
555 Broadway, New York, NY 10012-3999, USA.

Scholastic Limited
1-19 New Oxford Street, London, WCIA 1NU, England.

Scholastic Canada Limited
175 Hillmount Road, Markham, Ontario L6C 1Z7, Canada.

Scholastic Mexico
Bretana 99, Col. Zacahuitzco, 03550, Mexico D.F., Mexico.

Scholastic India Pte Limited
29 Udyog Vihar, Phase-1, Gurgaon-122 016, Haryana, India.

Scholastic Hong Kong
Room 601-2, Tung Shun Hing Commercial Centre,
20-22 Granville Road, Kowloon, Hong Kong.

Text © Annie Rae Te Ake Ake, 1999
ISBN 978-1-86943-388-8

15  14  13  12  11  10                    3 4 5 6 7 8 9 / 1

Edited by Penny Scown and Frances Chan
Designed by Frances Chan and Christine Dale
Cover by Khan Ahokava, oil on canvas
Artwork photography by Tony Nyberg
Typeset in 11/15pt Novarese by Egan-Reid Ltd
Printed in Hong Kong

# CONTENTS

# NEW ZEALAND
## Aotearoa (The land of the long white cloud)

## NORTH ISLAND
### Te Ika a Maui (The fish of Maui)

*The Legend of the Creation*

*Rona and the Moon*

*Rata and the Totara Tree*

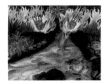

*Maui and the Fingers of Fire*

*Maui and the Sun*

## SOUTH ISLAND
### Te Waipounamu (The waters of the greenstone)

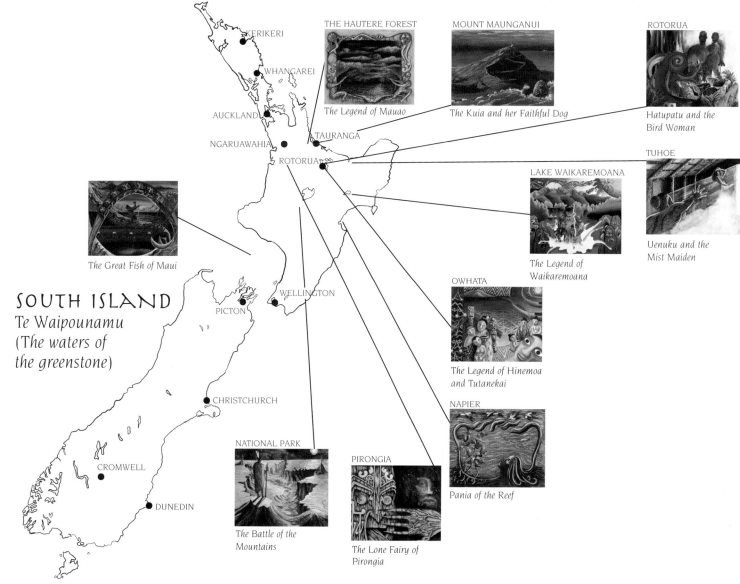

THE HAUTERE FOREST

*The Legend of Mauao*

MOUNT MAUNGANUI

*The Kuia and her Faithful Dog*

ROTORUA

*Hatupatu and the Bird Woman*

TUHOE

*Uenuku and the Mist Maiden*

LAKE WAIKAREMOANA

*The Legend of Waikaremoana*

OWHATA

*The Legend of Hinemoa and Tutanekai*

NAPIER

*Pania of the Reef*

PIRONGIA

*The Lone Fairy of Pirongia*

NATIONAL PARK

*The Battle of the Mountains*

*The Great Fish of Maui*

KERIKERI

WHANGAREI

AUCKLAND

NGARUAWAHIA

TAURANGA

ROTORUA

WELLINGTON

PICTON

CHRISTCHURCH

CROMWELL

DUNEDIN

4

# INTRODUCTION

Aotearoa, the Land of the Long White Cloud, was the name given to New Zealand by the Maori people.

Legend has it that the Maori made an epic journey from their ancient homeland of Hawaiiki, on seven sea-faring canoes, in search of new land. This long and arduous journey tested their faith, courage and endurance.

Early one morning, according to the legend, a young man who had been standing at the prow of his canoe staring out to sea, saw on the horizon a long white cloud. As the weary travellers drew closer to the cloud, it revealed a beautiful landmass that had lain hidden in the mists. They made this land their home.

These are some of the myths and legends of the Maori.

*Annie Rae Te Ake Ake*

# THE LEGEND OF THE CREATION

Before there was light there was darkness. Still and quiet it lay; a huge void; a vast nothing filled with the potential of all there was to be.

And the great void was profound, a limitless night. And deep in the blackness of that long night rested the creative thought, reaching away into forever, creating the earth and the sky.

Ranginui, the Sky Father, held Papatuanuku, the Earth Mother, in a close embrace. And there they lay, deep in the darkness of that long, black night.

Many children were born to them. The children lay cramped between their mother and father, deep in the blackness, longing for the freedom to move.

Tangaroa, the restless, the discontented, Tangaroa, god of the oceans to be, murmured in the darkness. "Let us part our parents."

There was a long silence. Then, with one voice, all but one brother whispered, "Ae, let us part them."

It was Tawhirimatea who did not speak. Tawhirimatea, the passionate, the caring, Tawhirimatea, god of the winds to be. Then he said quietly, "They are our parents. They gave us life. Leave them as they are. Let them be."

"And what kind of life is this for us," argued Tangaroa, "with no space to stretch our limbs, no space to explore the unknown? Again I say, let us part them!"

The brothers quarrelled. Bitterly they quarrelled. Alone in his view, Tawhirimatea was defeated.

It was decided that Tangaroa should be the first to try and separate Ranginui and Papatuanuku.

Impatiently he rose up. He heaved, he pushed, he shoved . . . and his parents clung tightly to one another, for great was their love. Finally, exhausted, Tangaroa sat down in the darkness.

Tanemahuta, the first-born, the courageous, the strong; Tanemahuta, god of the forests to be, spoke next. "Let me try," he said.

He lay with his shoulders pressed on his mother, and placed his feet on his father. He pushed, he pressed, he heaved and he struggled . . . and in the great darkness his parents lay, still bound together.

Tanemahuta the relentless, the tireless, kept pushing. He strained with every ounce of his being. "I can do it. I can do it . . . I *will* do it!" he thought to himself.

And slowly, very slowly, Ranginui was parted from Papatuanuku. Tane kept pushing until his father was away up high.

Ranginui wept as he looked down upon his beloved wife far below him. His tears formed the rivers, lakes and oceans. And Papatuanuku grieved for her exiled husband. The early morning mists are her silent tears.

Harley Carnegie

And thus did Tanemahuta, the remarkable, the endurer, separate his parents, Ranginui, the Sky Father, and Papatuanuku, the Earth Mother.

Light flooded into the world and for the first time the brothers looked upon their parents.

Tanemahuta then clothed his grieving parents. He dressed Papatuanuku in tall, stately trees, ferns, flowers and vines.

And Ranginui he dressed in rainbows, clouds, stars, the silver moon and the golden sun.

Tawhirimatea was sad. Tawhirimatea was angry. He swirled up and away, away from his brothers, up to join his father in the sky.

And to this day he remains there, aloof, for he remembers.

# UENUKU AND THE MIST MAIDEN

Dawn was breaking, and already Uenuku was deep in the bush. He was on his way to snare the fat kereru as they fed on the ripened miro berries. A light mist clung to the early morning bush giving the trees a shadowy, mystical appearance.

Suddenly, there in front of him stood the most beautiful young woman that he had ever seen. Their eyes met. The young woman looked bewildered and started to run away. Uenuku called softly after her, "Wait! I mean you no harm." She stopped and looked back.

"Who are you?" asked Uenuku. "Where did you come from?"

"My name is Hinepukoherangi, the maiden of the mist. I come here during the night to play in your bush-clad gullies and hills, and return to my home in the sky at dawn."

Uenuku was fascinated by the willowy mist maiden and begged her to stay.

"I cannot," she replied. "I must leave now,

for dawn is already on the earth. I shall return tonight when the mists come down."

Uenuku told her he would be waiting for her. And he was.

After several meetings, the young couple had fallen deeply in love. Hinepukoherangi agreed to become Uenuku's wife only if he promised never to tell anyone about her. She would spend every night with him and leave before dawn.

Uenuku agreed and they

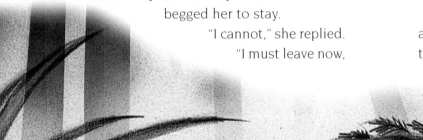

lived their secret life happily for some time. When a lovely little girl was born to them, Uenuku was very proud. His heart ached each day when he watched other children playing. If only they could see his own wonderful daughter, he thought. One day, in a weak moment, Uenuku boasted to his people about his lovely wife the mist maiden and his beautiful baby daughter. His people were curious to know more and suggested that he block up all the openings in his whare while his wife was asleep so that she might oversleep. They would then be able to see her for themselves the next day and know if he spoke the truth. In his eagerness to display his good fortune to his people, Uenuku did as they suggested.

That night, Hinepukoherangi awoke and said to Uenuku, "I dreamed it was time for me to go . . . and yet it is still dark."

"The night is not yet over," replied Uenuku. "Go back to sleep."

The second time Hinepukoherangi awoke, Uenuku urged her to go back to sleep again.

"It is indeed a long night," whispered the worried mist maiden.

The next time she awoke, Hinepukoherangi jumped up and rushed to the doorway. "Aue!" she cried, when she discovered the entrance was blocked. She pushed the barricade away and bright sunshine came pouring into the whare.

"You have deceived me, Uenuku!" she cried in dismay, and she flew away up into the air and disappeared.

Now Uenuku realised what he had done and he called to her, "Hinepukoherangi! I'm sorry! Please come back!"

His words went unanswered. It was too late.

Heartbroken, Uenuku travelled the land looking for his beautiful mist maiden. Over bush-clad hills and through steep gullies he wandered, searching for his beloved maiden from the sky. On some days he sat gazing at the clouds, remembering the joy he had once shared with the lovely Hinepukoherangi. But his long quest was in vain. She never did return.

At last, Ranginui, the Sky Father, took pity on Uenuku and changed him into a rainbow.

Sometimes, when the early morning mists are lifting from the earth, you may see a rainbow in the sky and you will know that Hinepukoherangi and Uenuku are together once more, watching over their descendants.

Daniel Yoon

# THE GREAT FISH OF MAUI

Away in a southern corner of the wide and expansive Pacific Ocean, there lies a land, shimmering in the morning sun. This land is known as Te Ika a Maui, and this is the story of why it is so named and how it came about.

Maui potiki was not liked by his older brothers. They were jealous of him and a little afraid of his magic powers, so they did not include him on any of their hunting or fishing trips.

One night, Maui overheard his brothers talking. They were going fishing the next day and were planning to leave early to avoid taking Maui.

Quickly, Maui made his way to his secret cave. He reached down behind a rock and pulled out his grandmother's magic jawbone. Cradling it in his hands, Maui trembled as he felt the power pulsing through it. This will be my hook, he thought to himself.

Silently he crept away to his brothers' canoe. He climbed in and hid under some flax mats that lay on the floor. Feeling pleased with himself, he soon fell asleep.

Before dawn the next morning, the brothers came creeping down to the beach. As silent as grey shadows, they got into their canoe and glided out on the dark waters. They did not see Maui, the trickster, hiding beneath their feet.

Maui waited until the brothers had paddled the canoe well out to sea, then he sprang from his cover.

"Kia ora, my brothers! It is I, Maui, your youngest brother! I have come fishing with you!" Maui grinned at their surprised faces.

Angry and resentful, the brothers grumbled among themselves. Meantime, Maui recited an ancient karakia and the canoe shot through the calm morning waters with the speed of a diving shag. The distance between the canoe and the land stretched quickly.

"Stop, Maui, stop!" shouted the brothers, clinging to the sides of the canoe, fearful for their lives.

When Maui stopped chanting, the land had disappeared from view and they were a long way out in the wide, rolling ocean.

"This is where we will do our fishing," announced Maui with a mischievous smile.

The brothers baited their hooks, but to teach Maui a lesson, they refused to give him any bait. Not to be defeated, Maui punched himself hard on the nose, and bright red blood tricked down his face. He smeared this blood onto the magic jawbone, which was his hook.

Standing up, he twirled his hook seven times above his head, then let it fly free. It soared up and out over the surging ocean, then hung suspended for a moment . . . before plunging down, down, down. Like a stone it fell, down into the green depths of the ocean. Down through the shadowy deep

it plummeted until, lodging itself firmly in the back of a magnificent fish, it stopped.

Maui felt the tug and began to pull in his line. He pulled and he strained. He hauled and he tugged. Far below him, the great fish began his fight, for he wished to remain in his watery home. He thrashed and dived, fighting bravely.

Maui shouted to his panic-stricken brothers. "Come and help me!"

But Maui's brothers clung to the sides of the bucking raft. The sea churned and rolled. Big waves rushed over the small canoe, thoroughly wetting the terrified brothers.

"Maui, release your line or we will all drown!" they pleaded.

But Maui, the endurer, was determined. Standing at the prow of the canoe, he closed his eyes and summoned up all his strength, his might, his will. "This I can do. This I can do," he told himself. He began chanting a karakia.

The line was taut and rigid as the magical words travelled down to the thrashing fish far below. The fish fought gamely but the ancient words were too powerful and soon, all his fight spent, the fish rose slowly to the surface.

And what a magnificent fish it was! There it lay, smooth and shimmering in the morning sun. Maui's brothers jumped onto the back of the great fish, their eyes wide with wonder.

Instructing his brothers not to damage the smooth back of the great fish, Maui dived down into the depths of the ocean to thank Tangaroa, god of the sea, for his marvellous catch, for this fish was one of Tangaroa's children.

But as soon as Maui had disappeared beneath the waves, his greedy brothers began arguing and fighting over which share of the fish was theirs. They fought and they shouted, and then they began cutting and hacking into that magnificent fish.

And wherever they cut great valleys and mountain ranges were formed. And in the countless years that followed, mighty trees and ferns grew on that great fish, and eventually people from across the ocean came to live on it. They called it Te Ika a Maui — The Fish of Maui.

And, even later, people from faraway countries came to live there too. They named Maui's fish the North Island of New Zealand. Perhaps you are living on this great fish's back . . .

# RONA AND THE MOON

High on a bush-clad hill above a peaceful valley was the home Rona shared with her husband and children.

At nights they delighted in listening to the sounds of the valley: a pair of ruru calling melancholy messages that echoed across the still blackness, a family of kiwi whistling to each other in high-pitched shrill voices, and the sound of Tawhirimatea, the wind, as he played in the leaves of the towering ancient giants that stood in the valley, daring to remember the dreams of another time. On long, twilight evenings, the joyful sound of the crickets and locusts rang out, filling the great valley with their music.

Rona and her family would watch the night sky as it became bejewelled in twinkling stars. They loved to gaze at Te Marama, the moon, enchantress of the night, as she walked the sky in her silver splendour. They were filled with awe as they watched her wax and wane, and then shrink to a mere slither before disappearing altogether.

Life at Rona's whare was peaceful and good.

Then one night, when the children were sound asleep and Rona was preparing to go to her own mat, Tirohia, her husband, wanted a drink of water. He went to the calabashes but they were all empty. What a commotion he caused. Normally a kind and considerate man, his impatient yells shattered the tranquillity of the night.

"Kahore he wai! Hei aha ai? There's no water! Why not?"

Was it not the job of the woman to fill the calabashes? He roared and complained until Rona could stand it no longer.

Taking an empty calabash, she headed down the track to the creek, muttering under her breath: "Am I the only person in the house capable of carrying water?"

And all the while, Te Marama gazed quietly down from her high vantage point.

The track was washed in moonlight as Rona tramped along, her thoughts prickly with indignation. The anger she felt was like a shield that hid the beauty of the night from her.

And so she went. Down past the kahikatea grove she strode. It was then that the world went dark! A great black cloud had moved across the face of the moon. Grumpily, Rona trudged on in the pitch blackness, feeling very sorry for herself.

The next thing she knew, her foot caught on a gnarly tree root and down she fell, flat on her face, giving her head a nasty blow. The calabash flew from her hand and smashed.

That was the final straw! Up she got, shaking her fist at the moon, who had just reappeared, cursing it with all her might: "Te Marama! Te wahine koretake! Upoko-kohua!" (which was about the rudest and worst insult you could say to anyone).

And away on high, Te Marama heard the curse of Rona, and chose to feel insulted. Down out of the sky she plunged.

"So you think I am good for nothing, do you? You think I should boil my head, do you?" hissed the angry moon.

She took Rona by the waist and pulled. Terrified, Rona clung to the ngaio tree. The moon tugged and jerked until she had wrenched the ngaio tree out of the ground. Up into the air they whirled with Te Marama firmly holding onto Rona who still clung desperately to the tree.

"I'm sorry! I didn't mean it! Please let me go!" wailed Rona. But her pleas fell on deaf ears.

They soared and sailed up to the home of Marama in the starry sky.

The next morning, as the sun rose golden bright above the blue mountains in the east, a troubled Tirohia gazed out of the whare. He was wondering what had become of his wife and now felt great remorse for his unreasonable behaviour the previous night. When his children awoke, they all went looking for Rona.

"E whaea, kei hea ra koe?" they called. "Mother, where are you?"

They hurried down the track that led to the creek. There they discovered the broken calabash, and saw where a tree had been uprooted from the forest floor.

It was then they heard Rona's voice calling from far away.

"Aue! Aue! Here I am! Up here! Up here in the moon . . ."

They looked up and, sure enough, there was Rona sitting in the moon, still holding onto the ngaio tree.

The children wept for their mother, afraid that she would never come back. And do you know, she never did!

If you look at the moon's face when it is full and round, you will see Rona still sitting there, lonely and wistful, still holding onto her tree.

16

*Stephanie Kim*

# THE LEGEND OF HINEMOA AND TUTANEKAI

Hinemoa was a puhi, a young woman of extraordinary beauty. Her admirers were many. She lived with her parents, Umukaria and Hinemaru, at Owhata on the shores of Lake Rotorua. Her father was the chief.

One day, her parents decided it was time for their daughter to be wed. They invited many chiefs from far and wide to a hui, letting it be known that they would be choosing a suitable and worthy husband for their daughter, the lovely Hinemoa.

There was great excitement in the air as the visitors sat down to eat. Hinemoa noticed a handsome young man among the guests.

"Who is he?" she asked her servant.

"That is Tutanekai, the young chief of Mokoia Island," she was told.

Tutanekai saw Hinemoa looking at him and smiled back at her. Her heart leapt with joy and in that instant she fell in love. When Tutanekai's servant came over with a message asking her to meet him down by the lake, she knew that he felt the same.

Hinemoa made an excuse to leave the gathering and hurried down the track that led to the lake. There, seated on a rock beside the waters of Rotorua, they declared their love for each other.

"Hinemoa," said Tutanekai, "I have a plan. If your father does not choose me to be your husband, come to me on Mokoia Island tonight, when everyone is asleep. Take one of your father's canoes."

"But how will I find my way in the darkness?" asked Hinemoa.

"There will be a full moon to light your way, and I will sit on the shore playing my flute," said Tutanekai. "My music will guide you safely to me."

Hinemoa agreed, and, eyes sparkling, the two young people slipped back separately into the wharekai.

Shortly afterwards, Chief Umukaria announced that he and his wife had chosen a husband for their daughter. Hinemoa's heart fell when she heard the name. It was not the handsome young chief from Mokoia Island.

Excitement replaced disappointment when she realised that the plan Tutanekai had suggested would be taking place in just a few short hours.

The merry-making had begun, poi swirled and many voices lifted in song. The man Hinemoa's father had chosen was not young, nor was he handsome, but he did have dominion over much land, and his people were many. He came and sat by Hinemoa, smiling. Hinemoa smiled back at him, daring not to look in Tutanekai's direction lest she give herself away.

As the last revellers left that night, Hinemoa lay down on her sleeping mat and pretended to sleep. She waited. When all was quiet in the wharenui, except for the occasional snore,

*Jung-Ah Lim*

she dressed in her finest feather cloak and stealthily made her way down to the lake.

She was unprepared for the sight that lay before her. The canoes had all been hauled high onto dry land! Her watchful father must have seen the looks that passed between Hinemoa and the handsome young chief. He'd had all the canoes dragged away up the beach to prevent his plans for a powerful marriage being thwarted.

Hinemoa was sorely dismayed. Desperately she tugged at one canoe, and then another, but she could not shift them.

She could hear the music of Tutanekai drifting across the water, calling her to him. Her heart surged with love. She knew now what she must do.

Creeping silently back to the pa, she took two hollow gourds and hurried back to the lake. Stepping out of her fine feather cloak, she placed the gourds under her armpits and waded into the cold waters of Rotorua.

Bravely, she began to swim towards the tiny island in the middle of the lake. Tutanekai's music lifted her spirits and she swam on. Marama, the moon, shone down making a silvery pathway on the water. The waters were cold but still Hinemoa swam on.

Suddenly, something cold and slimy took hold of her leg. She gasped. What was that? Could it be the dreaded taniwha who lived in the dark depths?

With fear threatening to engulf her, Hinemoa lowered her hand and cautiously stretched out her fingers to touch the creature that held her. Yes, she could feel the cold, hard scales. It must be the taniwha!

Gathering all her courage she spoke: "O taniwha of the lake, I am Hinemoa, daughter of Chief Umukaria of Owhata. I am swimming to Mokoia to marry Tutanekai. Please let me go!"

The taniwha listened to the words of the brave young woman and he felt compassion. He let go of her leg and slipped away into the darkened depths from whence he came.

Relieved, Hinemoa swam on.

Meanwhile, sitting in the sand on the beach at Mokoia, Tutanekai's eyes scanned the waters, looking for a canoe. Hinemoa should have been here long ago, he thought to himself. She must have changed her mind — or perhaps her father discovered our plan and stopped her from coming.

With a heavy heart, he stopped playing his flute and returned to the pa.

Hinemoa, alone now, with no music to guide and comfort her, swam on. Then Marama the moon disappeared behind a black cloud, leaving Hinemoa in the silent darkness. Bravely, she swam on.

At last, exhausted, her foot touched the sand, and she stumbled ashore and fell onto the beach at Mokoia. There she lay, face down, and rested.

On recovering she looked up and saw steam rising from

some rocks ahead of her. A hot pool! She went forward and lowered her cold, tired body into the warm waters.

Relaxing in the pool, Hinemoa realised that she had no clothes and suddenly felt shy. What could she do?

Presently she heard footsteps approaching, and hid in the shadows to watch. She saw Tutanekai's servant walk past carrying a calabash. He bent down to fill his container with water from the lake. Making her voice into that of a man's, she ordered: "Give me the calabash."

The servant was very frightened and looked wildly around for the owner of the voice. "Who are you? Wh-where are you?" he stammered.

Hinemoa stretched her hand from the darkness and the timid servant handed her the calabash. She raised it above her head and hurled it at the rocks. It smashed into a hundred pieces.

The terrified servant rushed back to his master. "A monster down at the lake demanded that I give him your calabash and then he threw it at the rocks!" he gabbled.

Tutanekai chuckled. "You don't have to invent stories to explain a broken calabash," he said. "Take another one — but this time be more careful."

The unwilling servant returned to the lake. Again Hinemoa changed her voice and demanded the calabash. Once more she flung it at the rocks, again shattering it into many pieces.

When the servant returned for a second time without the water, Tutanekai was angry. "I will go and get it myself," he said.

Hinemoa could hear footsteps approaching. These steps were bold and firm, not hesitant like that of the servant. She slid down deeper into the darkness of the rocks. Tutanekai

reached the lake and saw the remains of his two calabashes. Now he realised that his servant had spoken the truth.

"Come out and fight like a man, you breaker of calabashes! Stop hiding away like a lowly koura!" he roared.

There was no sound. Tutanekai reached into the darkness and grabbed hold of Hinemoa's hair. "Got you!" he yelled. He pulled, and out came Hinemoa.

Tutanekai was astonished. "It is you, Hinemoa!"

"Yes, it is I," whispered Hinemoa. She told him of her long, cold swim across the lake. She told him about the taniwha, and she told him of her shyness because she had left her clothes on the shore at Rotorua.

Tutanekai's eyes shone with love and admiration for his courageous Hinemoa. He gave her his cloak to wear and together they walked back to the pa.

The next day the people of Mokoia learned how Hinemoa had swum across the cold dark waters of Lake Rotorua for love for their chief. Proudly they prepared a celebration to honour the young lovers.

When Hinemoa's father awoke that morning and found his daughter missing,

he ran down to the lake. All the canoes were still high on the shore, and then he saw Hinemoa's cloak lying on the beach, and her footprints leading into the water.

She must have drowned herself, he thought, sadly. Oh my daughter! My beloved daughter!

He gathered a search party and they began to look for Hinemoa's body. All day they searched. When the search party neared Mokoia Island, they could hear the sound of singing and laughing coming from the pa.

Hinemoa's father's heart was very heavy as he anchored his canoe and went to tell Tutanekai the sad news. He could see that there was a wedding celebration in progress, so he

stopped, and waited.

But who was that sitting beside Tutanekai? It couldn't be . . .

Hinemoa stood, and looked at her father. There was a breathless hush. Then the chief of Owhata rushed forward and clasped his daughter to him. "Hinemoa, you're not dead! You're alive! My Hinemoa . . ."

He listened quietly as his daughter told him her story, then said, "You have proven yourself to be a very able and courageous young woman and I honour your choice of husband."

Having said that, Chief Umukaria gave the happy couple his blessing and with joy joined in the celebration.

*Clara Choi*

23

# RATA AND THE TOTARA TREE

Rata was still a youth. Everyday he watched the men of his tribe drag two canoes over the sand bar and paddle away into the open sea to the fishing grounds, and every night he saw them return. Although the two canoes would be laden with fish, it was barely enough to feed the many people of the tribe.

Rata sat and thought. There had to be a way to bring home more fish. At last he knew what he must do.

With the next sunrise, he would go into the great forest of Tane and find a suitable tree. He would chop it down and shape a canoe: a canoe that was strong and trustworthy; a canoe delicately carved, telling the noble stories of their ancestors; a canoe that would carry many men and a multitude of fish.

Before dawn, Rata arose and strode away into the great bush. He walked and walked until he came across the tree he was looking for. It was a giant totara, a magnificent tree that towered into the blue sky.

Rata began his toil. He chipped and chopped, chipped and chopped. The sweat poured from his brow, but still he kept working.

Near the end of the day, the mighty totara toppled to the ground with a great crash. Rata was pleased with his day's work and headed home.

Early next morning, Rata set off to begin work shaping the canoe. When he arrived at the spot, however, to his great astonishment he found the huge tree standing up straight and tall once more. Rata could not believe it. Did he only dream yesterday's work? It had felt so real!

Still puzzled, he began to chip and chop again at the large tree. As the sun was going down, the tree tumbled to the forest floor once more. Rata went home, weary and perplexed.

The next day, when he arrived back at the very same spot, there was the tree standing upright again, with every chip in place.

Now Rata knew someone was playing tricks on him, so he thought of a plan. He worked hard again all that day, and when the tree had fallen, he pretended to go home. Then he crept back and hid behind a fallen log, watching to see what would happen.

Very soon, he heard what sounded like singing and an amazing sight met his eyes. Thousands of birds and insects flowed out from the surrounding trees and began picking up the chips and putting them back in place. Behind them the patupaiarehe, the magical children of the night, sang and chanted magical karakia and the great tree slowly rose up and stood straight and tall once more.

Trembling with emotion, Rata leapt out from his hiding place, shouting: "Why are you doing this to me? Why?"

Shocked, the birds and insects and patupaiarehe looked up at the wild-eyed Rata.

"Because you did not ask Tane, god of the forest, for permission to chop down his tree," they said softly. "We are the guardians of the great forest."

Finally, Rata understood. He felt ashamed. In his haste he had not remembered the most important part of all. Sad, but wiser, he returned home.

The next day, Rata asked Tane, god of the forest, for permission to chop down the great totara so that he may build a canoe. A soft breeze sprang up and whirled around Rata's head and he knew that Tane had said yes.

This time, when the magnificent tree was felled, the birds and insects helped Rata hollow out the trunk and the patupaiarehe chanted karakia and carved nature's fine patterns in the red wood. This, indeed, was a mighty waka!

On his first voyage out to sea, Rata stood proudly at the prow and sent a silent thought of thanks to his forest friends. And from that day on, Rata never took another tree from the forest of Tane without first asking permission.

# THE LEGEND OF MAUAO

In those far off times, away up in the Hautere Forest, there stood three mountains. There was Otanewainuku, a chief, powerful and proud, a mountain of great mana. There was Puwhenua, a beauteous mountain with much grace. And the third mountain was of no importance, a nameless one, a nobody.

Although the nameless one was of no consequence, he had many friends, the magical children of the night — the patupaiarehe — and the birds and insects of the great forest of Tane.

One misty morning, as the nameless one was gazing across the gully, he noticed the rays of Te Ra, the sun, catching on the dewdrops that adorned Puwhenua's trees. They glistened and shone, and as the nameless one looked, he saw the beauty of his shy companion. His heart melted and he fell in love.

That night, as the silver light of Te Marama, the moon, shone down on the Hautere Forest, and as the stars twinkled away in the backdrop of forever, the nameless one asked his friends to take a message of love to Puwhenua, the lady who now occupied all of his thoughts.

But the patupaiarehe returned with news that shattered the hopeful mountain to the very essence of his being. The beautiful Puwhenua had eyes only for the great chief, Otanewainuku. Otanewainuku had captured her heart with his tall, majestic trees that stood a silent guard over his rugged slopes.

For a long while, the nameless one grieved for what might have been.

Finally, he called upon his many friends for help. He asked them to plait a special rope from the harekeke that grew in abundance down by the swamp.

This they did, and the plaintive sound of their karakia could be heard on the wind.

The nameless mountain gazed for the last time at the lovely Puwhenua. Behind her he saw the last rays of the sun painting the sky a bright red, framing his beloved in a fiery halo.

Sadly, he whispered, "Farewell," then quietly asked the children of the night to wrap the rope around him and drag him away . . . away down the valley to the Great Ocean of Kiwa

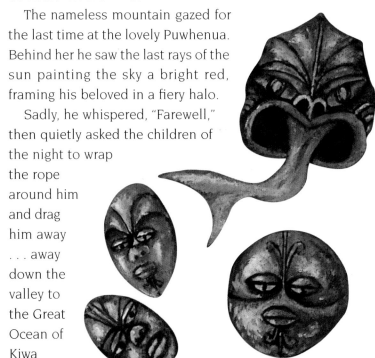

where he would sink beneath the waters and drown himself and so forget the pain of his unrequited love.

Full of sorrow, the patupaiarehe did as their friend bid and as the dark hand of night closed his fingers across the land, they began their arduous task.

With the chanting of karakia that brought the wisdom of the ancients forth, the nameless one began his long journey, down to the realm of Tangaroa, god of the sea.

A lonely morepork's cry echoed eerily in the dark night as the nameless one moved slowly away from his forest home. As he went, he carved out a river bed and his falling tears formed a river that flowed behind him. Down through the valleys and hills the tireless patupaiarehe dragged their forlorn friend.

Near the waters of Tauranga Moana, the sobbing of the nameless mountain became so great that, in despair, the patupaiarehe laid down their rope and waited for their sad companion to compose himself. Where they rested there now stands a pa, Waimapu, which means sobbing waters.

Then on, across the shallow waters of Tauranga Moana, the nameless one was dragged. The eastern sky was growing lighter as the patupaiarehe dragged their friend over a long sand bar.

Suddenly, with a great jump, up leapt Te Ra. His bright rays shot across the still waters, lighting up the wretched mountain. In terror and confusion, the patupaiarehe dropped the ropes and turned back towards the darkness of the Hautere Forest.

"Wait! Come back! Don't leave me here!" called the mountain with no name.

"Dear friend," the patupaiarehe called back. "The light of day has come and we must flee, for we are children of the night. But before we leave you forever, we shall give you dignity. You shall have a name. You will be called Mauao. Mauao, lit up by the first rays of the sun. Now we must leave you forever. E noho ra, dear friend, e noho ra!"

And they faded away, leaving Mauao standing at the end of a long, sandy spit. The urgent cries of the deserted mountain were lost in the sound of the breakers swirling and crashing around his feet.

And there he stood, a lonely figure gazing sadly out to sea, with his back to his home, the Hautere Forest.

Many years later, people from across the Great Ocean of Kiwa arrived on these shores. They bestowed an even greater name on him. They named him Maunganui, after a sacred mountain they had left far behind in their homeland of Hawaiiki.

*Mark Hansen*

# PANIA OF THE REEF

Karetaki was a handsome young man, tall and strong. He was greatly admired by all the young women from near and far, but Karetaki showed no interest in any of them.

One evening at dusk he was walking alone on a sandy beach, lost in thought, when he noticed a movement by some rocks. Curious, he stopped still and watched.

He thought he could make out the shape of a young woman, a maiden unfamiliar to Karetaki. Quietly, he moved closer to have a look. The girl's skin glistened with sea water and her hair lay black and shining on her back.

As Karetaki gazed upon her, he felt a warm stirring in his chest. The next moment the young woman turned, and gasped in surprise when she saw Karetaki.

"Do not be afraid. Come and talk to me," whispered Karetaki. She came shyly forward, and they gazed deeply into each other's eyes. Her eyes were as green as the seaweed, Karetaki noticed with surprise.

He gently took her hand and asked, "Who are you? Where have you come from? I have never seen you before."

The young woman looked out to sea and said, "I am Pania of the reef. My home is the wild ocean, my people are of the sea. Every evening my sisters and I come and play on these rocks. We watch the beautiful sunsets and we watch you from afar."

Now Karetaki understood why he had never seen her before. "I am Karetaki, and you are the most beautiful woman I have ever seen. Will you come and be my wife?"

"I cannot, I am of the sea. You are of the land."

They sat for a while on the warm, spray-soaked rocks, just looking at each other. Every so often, Karetaki would again invite Pania to share his life.

At last, she agreed to leave the sea and live on dry land with Karetaki, as his wife. Karetaki knew the pull of the sea would be very strong and he made Pania promise never to return to her people. He was afraid of losing his beautiful maiden to the sea.

Karetaki and Pania were very happy until one day Karetaki came to Pania and said, "I must leave you alone for a few days. It is time for me to hunt the fat kereru."

Pania begged her young husband to stay, but his mind was made up.

That night, as Pania lay alone on her bed, she listened to the sound of the breakers rushing in, and she could hear her sisters calling . . . calling her from the reef.

"Pania! Pania! Pania!"

Pania turned over and tried to block out the sound. But her sisters continued to call, over and over again. Very soon Pania found the longing too great and she left the whare and walked down to the sea. There were her sisters, all standing on the reef with their dark forms clearly

*Matt Wilmar*

silhouetted by the full moon, beckoning to her.

"Pania! Come and play with us!" they called.

"No," Pania replied. "I am Karetaki's wife now. I love him and can never return to my life in the sea. Please stop calling me. I have made my choice — I live on the land with Karetaki." And she turned back to the whare.

Her sisters called again. "Pania!"

Pania turned and looked back at her sisters.

"Come and have one last game with us," they urged.

One little game with my sisters won't hurt, Pania thought. My husband need never know.

She waded out into the sea where her sisters came to meet her. Joyfully they all dived and bobbed amongst the breaking waves. Then they rested out on the reef.

The eldest sister said, "Pania, our beloved parents have grieved since you left. Come down for a short visit. Your husband will never know."

Finally, Pania agreed. She agreed to return to the ocean depths for one last visit to her parents.

Down she plunged. Down . . . down . . . down . . . The cool water soothed her skin, and the little fish came up to greet her.

Pania wept for joy when she was reunited with her mother and father. She told them of her love for the man of the land, Karetaki. A shadow passed over her father's face.

That night, as Pania slept beneath the ocean, her father built a cage around her bed. When she awoke, Pania was filled with dismay. Her family had trapped her! She knew now that she would never be able to live up on the land with her husband Karetaki.

She wept bitterly and begged her parents to set her free, but they would not. "You belong here, Pania. This is your home. You are of the sea," they reminded her.

When Karetaki arrived home two days later, he realised at once what had happened. He rushed down to the beach and called for his wife.

"Pania! Pania! It is I, your husband Karetaki. Come home, my beloved. Please come home to me!"

And far below, Pania heard his desperate cry. She called back, but her soft voice was lost in the sound of the waves breaking on the rocks.

Night after night, Karetaki returned to the beach and sadly waited for his wife to return to him. But she never did.

When the moon is full on the glistening sea, sometimes Pania comes to the reef with her sisters. She gazes longingly at the land and her thoughts are with Karetaki. People say that at times you can hear Pania on the reef, calling, calling, ever calling . . . longing for the love of her husband, now lost to her forever.

# THE LEGEND OF WAIKAREMOANA

If you should linger on the shores of Waikaremoana, watching the waters rippling in the sunlight, you would never know the tumultuous origins of this usually peaceful lake. Come close now, and I will tell you. . .

In those ancient days long past, there lived a huge and terrible taniwha. His name was Mahu. He lived with his seven children, six of whom were also taniwha. The seventh child, the youngest, was human, and her name was Hau-mapuhia.

One day, Mahu was very thirsty and wanted water to drink. He called his children to him, saying: "I am thirsty. Take a calabash and get me some water. Go to the spring that is away beyond the great rock. There you can fill the calabash. Do not stop at the first spring, the nearest one, for that water is tapu — and tapu water must not be taken. Do you understand?"

Mahu's children complained, for they were lazy. But when their fearsome father roared at them, the six taniwha children hurried off. Hau-mapuhia did not go. She stayed home because it was too hot.

The way was long and the sun shone down fiercely. When the taniwha children came to the nearest spring, the spring of tapu water, they stopped and had a discussion.

"The sun beats down, and it is hot," complained one.

"Our father is a bully," sneered another.

"Let us sit and think," said a third.

They sat beside a log and watched the clear water gurgling up from the tapu spring. They watched as it slipped smoothly away over the shiny rock.

"Our father will not know the difference if we bring him back this water," said one.

"If we rest here for a while and watch the clouds, then return later with the water, he will think we've been to the spring beyond the great rock," reasoned another.

So . . . this is what they did. Much later, they returned to their waiting father. Mahu put the calabash to his lips and took a long, cool sip.

Spluttering, he spat out the water and turned on his wayward children: "This water is from the tapu stream! This water you have given me to drink is tapu! I shall punish you . . . I shall punish you like you've never been punished before. Stones you will all be — great smooth grey stones — and here you will stand forever! Until the end of time!"

Having said that, Mahu changed his six taniwha children into huge grey stones.

But still he was thirsty, so to his daughter, Hau-mapuhia, he went.

"I am hot, my daughter. My thirst is great. Go to the spring beyond the great rock and bring me water. Bring me water now!"

But Hau-mapuhia, who had always been her father's

favourite, said: "The day is hot, father, too hot for me, and the spring is too far. If you are thirsty, dear father, you must go to the great rock yourself, for I will not."

His daughter's words angered Mahu greatly. He turned to her threateningly.

"Once you had brothers and sisters," he hissed. "Now they all stand as stones."

Then a thought occurred to him. If he turned Hau-mapuhia to stone, he would have no children left. And having thought this, he relented.

To the spring beyond the great rock lumbered the great taniwha. He passed the tapu spring and on he went. The sun beat down relentlessly, and still he continued.

At last, he stood at the spring beyond the great rock. The cool water bubbled up from the earth and Mahu, hot and weary, drank deeply. But he was still angry.

"I do not care that Hau-mapuhia is now my only daughter. I *will* punish her," he said to himself. And he settled down to lie in wait.

Long shadows lingered on the earth as Hau-mapuhia awaited her father's return.

"Where is my father? Why does he not return?" she thought. "The black night will soon be upon us."

Finally, she decided to go in search of her father. Down to the spring beyond the great rock she ran. Night had fallen by the time she reached it.

"Father! My father! I have come to find you," called the small voice of the youngest daughter.

Out of the darkness jumped Mahu! He grabbed his youngest daughter. He pushed her under the water and held her there. Hau-mapuhia struggled and struggled. Still Mahu held her down. Hau-mapuhia became weaker and weaker as her life force ebbed away.

At that moment Tane, god of the forest, came by. He felt compassion for the young girl and turned her into a taniwha.

Hau-mapuhia felt her body change, then she felt a new strength course through her. With a great heave she pushed her father away. And still her body grew!

She became too large for the spring. Out she pushed, through the valleys and through the hills. She pushed the mountains aside and the water from the spring followed her. It gushed and spouted after her. She lunged and dived, and the water followed her wherever she went until it formed a huge lake.

Hau-mapuhia tried in vain to escape, but the disturbed and reckless taniwha was destined to remain. Wild waves dashed the shores. Water sprayed and foamed in the wake of Hau-mapuhia.

Hau-mapuhia is still there today. She has now turned to stone. She is long, she is smooth, she is grey. And the waters of Waikaremoana ripple through her lakeweed hair. The clouds look down in awe, and the trees stand guard in a stony silence.

Shane Evans

# MAUI AND THE FINGERS OF FIRE

Maui was a thinker. Maui was a trickster. Maui wanted to know.

One night, as he gazed into the flames of a brightly burning fire, he wondered how fire came to be. He sat and thought about this for some time. Every night, it was the job of the firekeeper to cover the last of the glowing embers with thick ash. In the morning the firekeeper would scrape away the ash and blow on the stored embers, placing a few dried twigs on them as he did so, until a flame leapt forth.

Maui wondered what would happen if the fire went out.

That night, when all around him were sleeping soundly, Maui quietly arose. He took a calabash of water and poured it over the stored embers. He heard a great sizzling sound . . . then all was quiet.

The next morning, the anguished shouts of the firekeeper awoke the village. "The fire! The fire! Someone has put out our precious fire! Aue! Who would do such a thing? What will we do?"

A large crowd gathered around the bewildered man.

Then Maui stepped forward. "It was I," he said.

A shocked hush spread through the pa. Taranga, the goddess, Maui's mother, approached him. "Why, Maui? Why did you do such a thing?"

"Because I wanted to find out where fire comes from," said Maui.

Sternly, Taranga said to her youngest son, "Maui, now you must go into the Underworld and find your grandmother, Mahuika. She is a fierce old lady, and out of her fingers shoots fire. You must tell her what happened and ask if you may have one of her precious fire fingers."

Maui set off. He crossed a gurgling stream that chattered over the stones, and watched his reflection moving in the clear water. Two friendly, flitting piwakawaka darted to and fro around his head. He travelled through gullies and over hills.

At last he reached the cave that was the entrance to the Underworld.

Down he climbed, out of the world of light. His eyes soon grew accustomed to the gloom. Away in front of him he could see a faint glow. That must be my grandmother, he thought.

As he drew nearer, Maui could see an old woman seated on a large stone. Tongues of flame shot from her fingers, lighting up the blackness. Her eyes gleamed like gimlets as she watched Maui approach.

"Tena koe, e kuia!" Maui greeted her. "You must be my grandmother, Mahuika, of whom my mother Taranga spoke."

The old woman peered suspiciously at Maui. "And what is your name?" she croaked.

"Maui-tiki-tiki-a-Taranga."

Mahuika nodded, then said, "It is a long journey for you to make. What is the purpose of your visit, Maui?"

"Grandmother, the fires in our village have gone out. Please

Debbie Milne

give me one of your fire fingers so we may enjoy the warmth and comfort of a fire on long, cold winter evenings? Please give me a fire finger so that we may cook our fish, our kumara, riwai and kereru?"

Mahuika snarled in the darkness. "So! You want one of my precious fire fingers, do you? What made your fire go out?" she demanded.

Maui hesitated. "Water was spilled on our stored embers in the night. Now we are without fire."

Hissing a curse under her breath, Mahuika took one finger of fire and thrust it at Maui. "Here. Take this fire finger . . . and mind you take good care of it!" she shrieked.

Maui thanked the old woman and set off towards home. He was crossing the creek that gurgled its way over the stones when he saw the bright flame reflected in the water below him. Maui laughed with glee as he watched the flame dancing in the water. So occupied was he in watching the reflection that he slipped on the mossy stones and fell into the creek.

There was a sharp, short fizzling sound and a wisp of steam rose from the fire finger. Maui laughed again. What a wonderful noise! "Sizzle, fizzle, sizzle!" he shouted.

Then he realised what he had done. Ooh! I must return to my grandmother and ask for another finger of fire, he thought.

Away down in the cave, Mahuika heard him coming, and she shrieked a curse that echoed in the hollow depths of her home.

"Why have you come back, Maui?" she screamed.

Maui stood with his head bowed, and answered, "Grandmother, I slipped on the smooth stones of the creek and fell into the water . . . the fire finger went out . . ."

"Careless boy! Useless mokopuna! I suppose you want another finger, eh? Do you? Eh?"

"Yes, I do grandmother," whispered Maui earnestly.

Grabbing another fire finger, the old woman threw it at Maui. "And mind you take good care of this one!"

Maui set off for home once more, determined this time to be a better caretaker. He was nearly home and was crossing the crystal clear creek when once again the reflection of the flaming fire finger caught his attention.

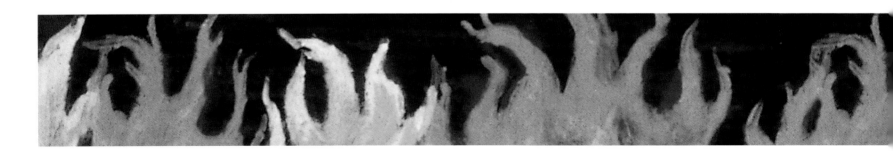

He stared at it. He moved his hand backwards and forwards, backwards and forwards, and the reflection danced in the waters of the creek.

Excited giggles rose up in Maui, and he began to create a dance of flames in the water below him. Again he stumbled and fell. And again the flame went out with a fizzle, hiss and steam.

Now Maui knew he was in trouble. Back he went to his grandmother in the Underworld. She tossed a fire finger at him and threatened terrible things should he return!

But, return he did, again and again . . . until she had given Maui all of her fingers, except one.

When Maui came back for the last time, his ferocious grandmother was waiting at the cave entrance. Screaming wildly, she lunged at Maui. He dodged her and ran back towards the bush. Her old legs weary with age, Mahuika knew she could not catch her nimble grandson and, pulling off her last finger, she hurled it with all her might at the quickly departing Maui.

The flames of her fire finger caught in the dry fronds of a ponga and leapt greedily up into the branches of the surrounding trees. Rapidly the flames spread, springing from tree to tree. Maui could feel the heat on his back and he could hear the crackling and spitting of the fire as it hurtled in pursuit.

Closing his eyes, Maui chanted a karakia that changed him into a kahu. Up he flew, away from the bush fire, to safety. His pleas for help were answered by Tawhirimatea, god of the winds. He sent storms to help quench the fiercely burning fire which was destroying the bush as it raced towards Maui's village.

The heavy rains quelled the raging fire, but before the last of it disappeared, Mahuika hid it in the heart of five trees: the kaikomako, the totara, the mahoe, the pate and the pukatea.

Maui saw his cunning grandmother do this from his vantage point in the sky. When she had disappeared back to the Underworld, he quickly took branches from these five trees and soon rekindled the fire.

Thus, Maui discovered the secret of fire. And today, fire is still found in these trees, if you know how to look for it.

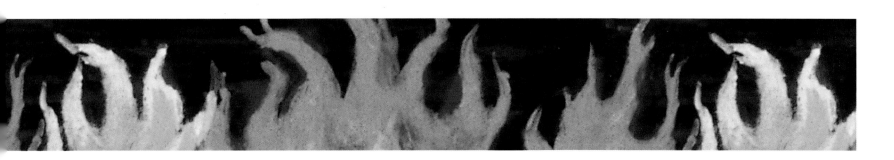

# HATUPATU AND THE BIRD WOMAN

Hatupatu was the youngest brother. This made him vulnerable to his older brothers' whims. And since they were jealous of the attention he got from their parents, the brothers took every opportunity to be mean to him.

One day, the two older brothers, Hanui and Haroa, were going hunting for birds and Hatupatu pleaded with them to let him come. Finally, they agreed.

Into the bush they tramped. When the three brothers reached a clearing, they set up camp. Hatupatu was told to stay there and keep guard. Hatupatu wanted to hunt too, but Hanui punched him roughly and ordered him to do as he was told.

Hatupatu spent the day at the camp, gathering firewood and preparing to cook the birds that his brothers would catch.

That evening, the older boys returned with three fat birds. Hatupatu's mouth watered as he smelled them cooking. But when the meal was ready, his brothers ate the birds, leaving only the bones for Hatupatu.

"We did all the work," they told him. "The bones are all you deserve!"

That night Hatupatu lay on his sleeping mat, his stomach rumbling with hunger.

The following day, Hanui and Haroa caught many birds, and Hatupatu was hopeful that he too might have one for himself. But, after eating their fill, the mean brothers gave Hatupatu only the bones, preserving the extra birds in bird fat.

Again Hatupatu went to bed hungry.

Next morning. When his brothers had gone off hunting, Hatupatu took a fat bird from the preserving pot, cooked it and ate it. He was so hungry, and it tasted so good, that he ate another one . . . and another . . . and another, until there were none left.

Feeling full and satisfied, Hatupatu lay down in the sun and slept.

When he awoke, the shadows were getting long and Hatupatu knew that his brothers would soon be returning. He realised only too well what he had done. His brothers would indeed be angry. What would he tell them?

From his desperation an idea blossomed. Quickly, Hatupatu threw the cooking pots around, scattered the wood, then punched himself in the nose until it bled. Then he lay down in the middle of the mess with his eyes closed.

Presently his brothers returned. Hatupatu pretended to regain consciousness on hearing their voices. He proceeded to tell them about the band of warriors that had attacked their camp and taken the birds, beating him when he tried to stop them.

Surprised, the brothers tidied up the camp and cooked their day's catch, again giving Hatupatu only the bones. Then they stored the remaining birds in fat and settled down on

*Reihana Pene*

their mats for the night.

But Hanui was suspicious of Hatupatu's story. He whispered to Haroa in the darkness: "Did you notice our young brother, Hatupatu? He did not look so hungry tonight. He did not plead with us to give him some meat, and he did not fall on the bones as ravenously as usual. All is not well, my brother."

The next morning, Hanui and Haroa pretended to go off hunting, but instead they doubled back and hid, watching the campsite. Hatupatu hurried to the preserving pots and busied himself cooking the birds. He had just begun his fine feast when his brothers sprung from cover.

"You deceitful little thief!" they yelled. "It is you who has been eating our birds!"

And with that, they picked up large sticks and rushed at Hatupatu, intent on punishing him severely.

Hatupatu, full of fear, leapt up and raced away into the bush, his angry brothers chasing after him. So angry were they that when at last they caught him, they beat him to death!

They covered his body with the feathers of the plucked birds and departed. They returned to their parents, and told them that Hatupatu had not listened to them and strayed away from camp. They said that now poor Hatupatu was lost in the great forest of Tane.

Their wise parents, suspecting all was not well, sent the spirit of an ancestor to search for Hatupatu. The spirit, taking the form of a blowfly, quickly found the body of Hatupatu lying beneath the feathers and by chanting an ancient magic spell, brought him back to life.

On awakening, Hatupatu sat up to find that it was now dusk and already the bush was dark and shadowy. The still silence was suddenly broken by the sound of giant wings flapping and Hatupatu saw a huge flying creature land on a branch above him.

It was grotesque, having the body of a bony woman and the beak and wings of a bird. Its claws were long and very sharp. The huge, ugly creature peered at Hatupatu, who lay still, hoping that she would not see him.

But it was not to be. With a shrill screech, she spread her large wings and glided down to Hatupatu. Clasping him in her giant claws, she lifted him and flew off over the darkening bush.

Very soon she landed on the upper branches of an enormous rimu tree, and Hatupatu could see a huge cage with many birds inside. The Bird Woman opened the door of the cage and pushed Hatupatu in roughly. Then she locked the door and flew off into the night.

What was going to happen to him? Hatupatu wondered. Why had she thrown him into this cage with all these birds? What were they doing here? He looked around. There were seven kereru, eight kaka, five tui and six plump piopio. A pipiwharauroa hovered close by, above the cage.

It was cold, and Hatupatu found sleep evaded him.

Early in the morning the Bird Woman returned. She peered into the cage and opened the door, screeching, "Now, who is going to feed Kurungaituku today?"

Taking hold of a bright green

kaka, she stuffed it into her great, cavernous mouth, and with a couple of crunches she'd swallowed it and spat out a few feathers. Then she locked the door once more and flew away.

Now Hatupatu had the answers to his questions. They were all to be food for that great ugly creature. He must get away. Hatupatu studied the lock, then took a twig from the rimu and set to work on it.

The sun was high in the sky when the door of the cage sprang open.

"Come!" said Hatupatu to the birds. "Fly away quickly."

All the while the pipiwhareroa was perched on a high branch watching. "Ko-ri-ro! Ko-ri-ro!" she called in her shrill, piercing voice as the birds all flew to safety. Hatupatu climbed down the tree and began to run. The spying pipiwhareroa flew swiftly away to find her terrible mistress.

As Hatupatu ran, he could hear the angry screams of the giant bird and the loud flapping of her powerful wings as she found his scent and pursued him. Although his legs were tired, Hatupatu sped on, not daring to rest while the horrible sound of the flapping wings got closer and closer.

Desperately, Hatupatu searched for a place to hide. He came upon a huge rock and addressed it with passion: "Oh rock, who has stood here since the beginning of time, please open this day and give me refuge!"

And the rock opened. Hatupatu rushed in and the rock promptly closed behind him just as the fearsome Kurungaituku swooped down. Angrily she clawed and pecked at the rock. She shrieked and screamed, and her cries were ringing through the bush, making everything afraid.

But the rock stood firm. It did not open.

After a fierce assault, the Bird Woman drew back to wait and rest and to think of a plan. Night came, and still the rock did not open. Kurungaituku watched and waited.

In the early hours of the morning, Hatupatu peered out and saw that the terrible creature had nodded off. Whispering his gratitude to the rock, he stepped out and crept past his sleeping enemy.

He was hurrying quietly through the bush when he heard Kurungaituku's spy, the pipiwhareroa, fly past him crying, "Ko-ri-ro!"

Hatupatu ran wildly now, running for his life! As he ran, he heard the piercing screams of the Kurungaituku.

"I, Kurungaituku,
will catch this meddling human,
and I, Kurungaituku,
this day will devour him
and spit out his bones!"

Fear leant speed to Hatupatu and he sped frantically towards his home. He could hear the shrieks and screams of the Bird Woman getting closer all the time.

Ahead he could see the stream of hot pools and he could hear the plopping of the thick, hot mud. He dashed towards the mud pools and leapt across the bubbling mass just as Kurungaituku rushed up.

So intent on her prey was she that she didn't see the boiling mud. Splat! She fell face first into the pool. Her screams were terrible and she struggled, flopping and turning and scrambling in a vain attempt to free herself from the scolding death-trap. Down she sank, deeper and deeper, until she disappeared beneath the boiling mud.

With great relief, Hatupatu thanked the pool for its help, and walked on home.

His parents were overjoyed to see him, and his two jealous brothers, on seeing Hatupatu come back from the dead, were so fearful of him that from that day forward they never gave him any more trouble!

Martin Mihaka

# THE LONE FAIRY OF PIRONGIA

The shrill screech of a lonely morepork echoed along the valley, piercing the stillness of the black night.

A lone patupaiarehe walked stealthily down from his mountain home, towards an isolated whare on the outskirts of a village.

Sitting inside the whare, poking the glowing embers of her fire, was the beautiful Te Whaitu. Her son, Tama, lay sleeping at her feet. Her husband, Ruarangi, was away on the ridges snaring birds to store away in preparation for the cold winter days ahead.

Te Whaitu was lost in thought, remembering her other son, Rangi, who had gone into the long night, the black night of death, beyond the veil. She still grieved for him, this one that had taken the path into the next world.

She did not see the lone fairyman, standing in the darkness, peering at her through the open door. She looked up startled when he entered, and shouted loudly as he picked her up and ran off, carrying her towards the higher slopes of Mount Pirongia.

There he gave her a strange drink . . . and the beautiful Te Whaitu forgot all about her family.

Next morning when Ruarangi returned, he found Tama huddled in the whare, his face stained with tears, weeping bitterly.

"Why do you cry?" he asked his son. "Where is your mother?"

"In the deep of the night, a patupaiarehe burst in and carried her off! My mother shouted and struggled, but to no avail," Tama cried sadly.

In despair Ruarangi huddled down beside his son, and he also wept. He wept for the loss of his beautiful wife, Te Whaitu.

He looked up, and there, standing by the ridge pole was an apparition, pale and ghostly. It was the spirit of his dead son Rangi.

The apparition spoke: "I see you both in a huddle. I see you both weeping. What misfortune has befallen my family? And where is my mother, Te Whaitu?"

Ruarangi told him about Te Whaitu being carried off in the night by a lone patupaiarehe.

Again, the apparition spoke: "Stop weeping now! Stand up! There is much for you to do. Listen carefully and do as I say and Mother will return to you.

"Go towards the rising place of the great Ra. You will come to a river. This river is wide. This river is shallow. It flows over a bed of shiny smooth stones. Up above, on a plateau, rises a mound of large boulders. You will hear voices calling to you. Do not stop! Pay no heed! You must go on.

"Further on, you will come to another river. This river is narrow. This river is deep. It flows swiftly, dashing over logs, roaring through rocky ravines. You will find a log spanning the width of this treacherous waterway. Cross there. Again you will hear voices. Do not stop! Pay no heed! Go on.

*Tukukino George*

"When you come to the third river, stop! A plump kereru will come flying by. Catch this bird. Prepare it for cooking. Stuff it with ripened miro berries. Cook it over the flames. Let the sweet aroma waft freely around. And sit down and wait. Just wait.

"Do as I say, and Te Whaitu will return."

With this the ghostly figure of Rangi disappeared.

Ruarangi and Tama set off immediately. They crossed the wide, shallow river with the smooth stones that shone and gleamed in the sunlight. They saw the big boulders on a plateau. They heard voices calling to them. They paid no heed. They went on.

They came to the second river, the narrow, deep river. They heard the roar of the water as it rushed through the rocky ravine. They found the log spanning the width, and crossed over. Voices called to them, but they paid no heed. They went on.

At the third river they stopped. They made a fire. They caught the kereru that came flying by and prepared it for cooking, stuffing it with miro berries. They cooked it over the flames. They sat down. They waited, they watched, they listened.

The pungent smell of the bird cooking wafted through the air, and was carried on the breeze to faraway places.

Away up on the slopes of Pirongia, the meaty aroma reached Te Whaitu's nose, breaking the spell that had been cast upon her. Big tears welled up in her eyes as she remembered her beloved husband Ruarangi and son Tama.

Following the smell of the cooking bird, Te Whaitu finally came across Ruarangi and Tama waiting for her. Great was the family's joy as they were reunited.

Te Whaitu then warned them that the patupaiarehe would soon be returning and would learn of her escape. They must hurry!

That night, the ghostly figure of Rangi reappearred beside the ridge pole of the whare. This time, he told them: "Take some fat of the kereru and mix it with red ochre, then spread it over all the buildings on the marae. Leave only the ridge pole of the whare untouched. Do it now — quickly — before the fairyman discovers his loss."

The ghost of Rangi faded once more, and his family hastened to do his bidding. Ruarangi mixed the bird fat with the red ochre, and together they spread it over all the buildings of the marae. When the task was completed they settled into the wharenui to sleep.

In the early hours of the morning, a piercing cry was heard, coming from the higher slopes of Pirongia. A solitary figure hurried down the side of the mountain in search of Te Whaitu.

When he reached the marae he stood a short way off, perplexed, not knowing what to do next, afraid of the red fat that smelt like the food of a human.

But his desire for the beautiful Te Whaitu was great. Summoning courage, he felled a tree and leant it against the untouched ridge pole of the whare. He scrambled up the trunk and searched desperately for a way in. He looked this way and that, his thin, bony hands tearing at the sturdy pole. But the pole was strong and would not yield.

And all the while the strong smell of the cooked bird fat wafted up his nostrils, sickening him.

Finally, defeated, he gave a loud shriek, slid down the ridge pole and fled into the black night, never to be seen again.

*Behold, a cold south wind blows across the land*
*as the stranger leaves*
*never to return to that valley.*
*And from far away*
*a thin, plaintive wail rides the wind*
*to places high and low*
*as a lone patupaiarehe fades away,*
*becoming lighter than cobwebs,*
*disappearing into thin air.*

# MAUI AND THE SUN

Once, a long time ago, Te Ra the sun did not travel slowly across the sky as he does today. The people were not happy, for they did not have the time to do all they wanted to do. The sun would jump up and run across the sky before disappearing behind the western hills, leaving Earth clothed in another long, dark night.

The fishermen grumbled because they had no time to do their fishing. The hunters moaned because they had no time to hunt the fat kereru. The women grizzled because they had no time to weave their baskets and mats. And the children cried because they had no time to play.

Everyone was discontented. "That sun goes too fast, " they complained. But no-one knew what to do.

Then Maui said, "I will go to Ra and order him to slow down."

Maui asked the wise women of the tribe to gather harakeke at the dawning of the next day — and to plait a special rope. This they did — and as they worked Maui recited a karakia, to give the rope the extra strength and durability that he needed. Then he gathered together the strongest and bravest of the tribesmen, and asked them to go with him to capture the sun. He explained that this journey would demand the greatest of courage and that his men would need to muster up all of their inner strength.

Soon Maui and his gallant band of men were ready, and as dusk was falling, he led them away towards the east.

They travelled only in the dead of the night so Te Ra would not see them coming. During the day, Maui and his men curled up and slept under ferns and logs to keep out of the gaze of the hurrying sun. Every night they walked on and on until at least they reached the very edge of the world.

Maui found the huge hole from which the sun sprang each morning. He and his men made a snare using their special ropes. They set the trap over the hole and in the darkness they sat down to wait.

As dawn approached, a red glare could be seen away down in the depths of the hole. Maui began chanting karakia to protect himself and his brave men. The light grew brighter and brighter as Ra came closer.

Suddenly, the sun jumped up!

"Pull!" ordered Maui, and the men pulled, and the net fell over the astonished sun.

"Aue! What is this?" roared the sun. "What are you doing? Let me go!"

"Hold tight, men!" shouted Maui as he leapt forward and begun to beat Ra with his mere.

The sun screamed in pain. "Whoever you are, I command you to release me immediately!"

"No!" shouted Maui, and he continued to beat Ra.

The sun writhed in agony. "Why are you doing this to me?"

*Anita Best, Junita Browman, Elisha Bunn*

51

he moaned. "Why do you beat Tama-nui-te-Ra?"

"Because you travel too quickly across the sky," replied Maui. "If you promise to slow down, we will let you go."

"Why should I?" said the sun sulkily, and Maui started beating him again.

Ra writhed in agony, but could not escape the determined blows of Maui.

"Alright! Yes! I promise!" he agreed. "I will travel more slowly."

Maui lowered his mere. "We have an agreement then! Be warned that I will be back if you break your promise."

The men released the ropes and the sun rose slowly into the sky, too weak from his beating to go any faster. And when Maui and his men returned to the tribe they found the people rejoicing in the longer days.

But now and then Ra forgets to travel so slowly and he hastens his pace just a little. We call this time winter, when the days are shorter. But when he recalls the beating Maui gave him, Ra slows down again and the long, warm days of summer return to the land.

# THE KUIA AND HER FAITHFUL DOG

Beside the foaming ocean they lived, this kuia and her dog. They were the best of friends and were inseparable.

As the first light played on the eastern horizon, the two of them could be found wandering along the white sands of Maunganui, watching the seagulls wheeling over the sea. They watched the birds gliding effortlessly over the morning waters, searching, peering into the ocean depths, then diving like arrows onto their unsuspecting prey.

At times, the old woman and her beloved pet would sit in silence on the sand dunes at dawn, listening to the murmuring of the sea and watching the colours of the clouds change from royal purple to flaming red as the great Ra rose up out of the ocean to begin his march across the sky.

Then the kuia and her dog would clamber out over the big rocks to the promontory that jutted like a pointing arm into the rolling ocean. There, the waves rushed into a rocky cauldron, roaring and crashing, then breaking into frothy white foam as they dashed wildly around searching this way and that for a way back to the arms of their great parent, the Ocean of Kiwa.

The dog would snuggle up against his mistress and close his eyes as the old woman gently stroked his head and sang him the ancient songs of her ancestors.

The tribespeople honoured the old woman by seeing that both she and her cherished dog were well fed. They would watch the dog and his mistress wandering along the beach and would say: "They are indeed a fine pair, like a fish is to water."

One morning, when fine mists were covering the topknot of Maunganui, this adventurous couple set off to climb through the clouds to sit on the top of this seaside mountain. They wanted to look out over the ocean, the harbour and surrounding lands.

Up they climbed, the old woman slowly shuffling along, stopping every now and then to rest. The way up the mountain was steep and their path led them along sheer cliff faces which dropped away to the moaning sea below. But they were careful, and stepped surely along the high, stony path.

A little piwakawaka flitted above their heads, darting to and fro catching the small flying insects that had been disturbed by the early morning walkers. Every now and then it would perch on a branch up ahead, waiting, its fan-shaped tail flicking this way and that.

Up through the mists they climbed. Tiny droplets of water gathered on the dog's coat and in the kuia's hair. Trees and shrubs shone dark green in the misty light, and the world below them disappeared from sight.

Higher and higher they climbed, until at last there they were, on top of the clouds, standing on the mountain's peak. The brilliant sunshine dazzled them, its beams catching in the cobwebs that hung from nearby manuka.

The kuia stroked her dog's head and told him stories of the Creation, a long way back at the beginning of time. The dog listened with his eyes shut, happy in the warmth of his mistress's love. Thus they sat for a long time.

When the kuia looked again, she noticed that the mist had cleared. Below them the great expanse of blue ocean sparkled and gleamed in the morning sun. Behind them, in the distance, lay the smoky grey-green hills of the Hautere Forest. Looking to the north, along the shoreline of Matakana Island, the old woman saw something that sent a cold shiver down her back.

There, in the lee of the land, she saw a great long canoe approaching — a canoe filled with many men. This canoe was unfamiliar to the kuia. This canoe looked like a war party paddling silently along the coast towards her village. A war party coming to attack her people! She must warn them!

Jumping to her feet, the old woman began hobbling as fast as she could down the mountain. The dog, sensing his mistress's distress, gave a whine and hurried after her.

Down they went at great speed, the old woman reciting an ancient karakia as she ran. Down through the trees they careered, the old woman now calling at the top of her voice: "A war party is coming! A war party is coming!"

As they came upon the path that led along the cliff face, the tired old legs of the kuia stumbled, and she fell. Down, down she tumbled, right over the edge of the cliff.

Her faithful dog was left at the top of the cliff, yelping and whining as he watched his beloved mistress fall into the churning sea far below. Over the cliff he leapt, yelping as he fell, plummeting down into the unyielding sea. Although slightly stunned, he resurfaced, his eyes searching for his kuia.

He found her lifeless body lying face down in the sea with her grey hair floating around her head like seaweed. He swam to her and took the kuia's hair in his mouth, trying to hold her head out of the water. He stayed with her until the great sun had disappeared behind Matakana, then, exhausted, he finally let her go and they both sank beneath the surface.

Tangaroa, god of the sea, had witnessed the old woman's efforts to save her people and had seen the dog's heroic struggle to save his mistress, and he was moved. He looked upon their lifeless bodies lying side by side and felt compassion for them.

"A love such as theirs shall be remembered," he vowed, and thus saying he turned their bodies into rock.

There they stand to this day, side by side to the north of the mountain known as Maunganui. The bigger rock is the kuia and the small rock her dog. They stand in the sea at the entrance to the Tauranga harbour. The old woman's hair still floats around her. Some call it seaweed.

When fishermen pass these rocks they throw food to the old woman. This pleases Tangaroa, and the fishermen hope that it will bring them good luck as they fish in the Great Ocean of Kiwa.

Yi-Chang Lin

# THE BATTLE OF THE MOUNTAINS

The great mountain Tongariro felt uneasy as he looked across the gap at the scowling faces of Taranaki, Tauhara and Putauaki. He knew they were about to challenge him for the love of Pihanga.

Pihanga stood straight and still, sad at the situation that was brewing, for gentle was the nature of this beautiful lady who wore the fragrant cloak of the pikikaiarero.

Meanwhile, Ruapehu and Ngauruhoe played, happy in the innocence of childhood, oblivious to the mounting tension around them.

The restless mountains hovered nearby, each preparing to claim Pihanga as his bride. But Tongariro stood in their way.

Tongariro, the tuakana, the eldest, watched, his eyes steady as each of the rival mountains stepped up and issued their challenge. Then, with the formalities over, the war began!

Loud rumblings rattled from deep inside of Taranaki. The ground shook with his passion, and out of his topknot flew red-hot rocks that careered straight at the waiting Tongariro.

Retaliating immediately, Tongariro let out a deafening roar and sent boulders of fire hurtling back at Taranaki. Putauaki and Tauhara, seeing their chance, came from behind while Tongariro's attention was diverted. Great flows of boiling lava came spilling out of their craters and rushed wildly at Tongariro's back.

Pihanga's warning gasp alerted the agile mountain, who quickly side-stepped the boiling rivers of volcanic spew.

The battle raged on. The earth shook and the air was thick with sulphurous fumes. Fierce was the fight for the beautiful Pihanga.

A mighty blow from Taranaki sent the topknot of Tongariro flying through the air and it landed with a tremendous splash in the great lake nearby. And still the defending mountain fought back, for great was the courage and endurance of the noble Tongariro. And, at the end of the day, it was these qualities that finally won through.

Sorely beaten, the three challengers used the cloak of the night to make their retreat. The two youngest mountains headed away towards the east. Tauhara, the romantic, kept looking back to catch one last glimpse of the lovely Pihanga. He knew now that she could never be his wife. He reached no further than the northern end of the great lake Taupo -nui-a-Tia.

Putauaki travelled much more swiftly, for he wished to put much distance between himself and his lost love. He journeyed to the very end of the flat lands of Kaiangaroa, where he still stands, a lonely sentinel of the Bay of Plenty.

Taranaki, much older, and having much more pride to deal with, wanted to suffer his defeat in private. He turned and headed westward, to the place of the setting sun. In his haste to get away he gouged a deep furrow down which began to flow the Wanganui river.

On seeing his opponents leaving, Tongariro let out a loud blood-curdling scream, a mighty cry of victory that echoed out through that dark night.

Taranaki, thinking that he was being pursued by his victor, called upon the wisdom of the ancient realms to help him.

Up he rose, and through the air he soared to a spot far away in the west. And at this very moment, the first rays of Te Ra came skipping over the landscape, transfixing the fleeing mountains.

At a safe distance, and still bristling with resentment, Taranaki turned and hurled stinging insults at Tongariro.

And across the great distance that now lay between them, Tongariro heard the insults of Taranaki and felt sad, for he well remembered the friendship they had all shared in their childhood.

Seeing the grief of her beloved companion, Pihanga sent soft clouds of love to embrace and soothe him, for great was the love of this gentle lady.

And over the years, the bond between them has been steadfast, and they stand side by side to this very day.

# ABOUT THIS BOOK

Every society has its own myths and legends as a means of explaining the unexplainable, especially to its young people. The oral myths and legends of Maoridom — *nga taonga tuku iho nga tupuna* — exist as a strongly unifying influence within their midst. They are generally well-known and regularly referred to, particularly within the context of the natural environment upon which they overlay a special spiritual dimension.

Scholastic New Zealand brings this collection of Maori myths and legends together with the talents of secondary school artists, the first book of its kind in this country. The artists are of Maori, European, Pacific Island and Asian descent, drawn from schools throughout New Zealand. Each has been given the task of interpreting a story in their own way. So this book is not only a retelling of ancient stories but a presentation by a representative group of this nation's young people responding to the foundational myths of their New Zealand culture. As an expression of their nurturing cultural environment, it shows the vigour of young people and their sensitivity to those mystical forces which surround them.

Without question, respect and recognition must be given to Annie Rae Te Ake Ake for her gift of storytelling, and the secondary school art teachers who supervised and guided their students in this project.

Traditional stories are passed on from generation to generation. There is a Maori saying that such stories are not the possession of any one person but, like love, are important to be held in trust, with a responsibility to pass them on — *tuku iho, tuku iho* — to the next generation.

*Roger Hardie*
Art Co-ordinator

# ABOUT THE AUTHOR AND ILLUSTRATORS

Annie Rae Te Ake Ake lives with her family in Oropi, 19 kilometres from Tauranga. Her iwi affiliations are with Ngati Ranginui, Ngai Te Rangi, Ngati Maru and Ngati Tuwharetoa.

This is her first book and it came about through her love of storytelling. On request from her mokopuna, Annie made a home recording of some favourite legends on tape. Three volumes were later recorded in a studio, entitled *The Boat Shed*, and these were marketed to schools in New Zealand. School teachers then asked Annie for written copies of these ancient stories. Thus began the demanding task of transcribing the stories and the manuscript for *Myths and Legends of Aotearoa* was born. Now she is delighted to see her stories become a beautiful picture book with the help of many young, talented artists.

At present she and her sister Gay, her daughter Tania, and her daughter-in-law Karen, run a full-time business creating, publishing and marketing educational resources for schools.

Annie is a life enthusiast. She enjoys walking in the bush, poetry, singing, white water rafting and good red wine. She reads widely on topics concerning ancient wisdoms, sciences, the nature of reality, human biology and consciousness, religions and mythologies.

Annie has begun writing her next series of myths and legends and she has also started a collection of childhood memories, as short stories of her whanau.

**The Legend of the Creation** — *acrylic on paper*
Illustrated by Harley Carnegie (16), Tikipunga High School, Whangarei

Harley's painting shows Ranginui and Papatuanuku "detached in an almost tomblike state. Tanemahuta is in the middle heaving his parents apart. Tawhirimatea is blowing from the left, trying to subdue his rebellious brothers." In 1999 Harley plans to complete Bursary Art in painting, printmaking and sculpture and would like to do a jewellery course. He also likes surfing, snowboarding and skateboarding.

**Uenuku and the Mist Maiden** — *watercolour, airbrush and coloured pencil on paper*
Illustrated by Daniel Yoon (19), Burnside High School, Christchurch

Born in Korea, Daniel plans to continue studying art at the Wellington School of Design or Canterbury University. He also enjoys singing, music and playing ice hockey.

**The Great Fish of Maui** — *oil on canvas*
Illustrated by Khan Ahokava (16), Papakura High School, Auckland

Auckland-born Khan comes from Tongan-German descent. In his illustration he is "trying to show a summation of all the events that took place in the myth, especially the cultural atmosphere." Khan enjoys painting in oils and drawing, particularly in earthy colours, and also likes to design wearable art items. He hopes to follow a career in design, illustration or architecture. Khan's sporting interests include surfing and skateboarding.

**Rona and the Moon** — *acrylic and coloured pencil on card*
Illustrated by Stephanie Kim (17), Glenfield College, Auckland

"As soon as I finished reading the story, I pictured a peaceful landscape, but behind this beautiful night scene, a somewhat sad woman reflected in silver moonlight appeared in my thoughts." Born in Korea, Stephanie attended the prestigious Sun Hwa Art School for three years before moving to New Zealand. She is also studying English, Japanese and French, and is interested in many art-based careers including illustrating, architecture, designing and movie directing. "But my final goal is to become an art historian who can truly understand 'art'".

**The Legend of Hinemoa and Tutanekai** — *oil on canvas*
Illustrated by Clara Choi (17) and Jung-Ah Lim (17), Northcote College, Auckland

Painting, printmaking and design are Clara's favourite subjects "because we get to express our own ideas." As well as having a keen interest in art, Seoul-born Clara also has plans of becoming a lawyer. Her other interests include playing piano and kendo.

Jung-Ah, also from Korea, is another young artist developing her use of media in painting, printmaking and 3D design. Jung-Ah plans to study at Auckland University's Elam Art School and eventually work as an artist.

**Rata and the Totara Tree** — *acrylic and ink on paper*
Illustrated by Nick Sydney (17), Logan Park High School, Dunedin

"I was pleased to illustrate this story because I remember it from my childhood. It was a story that everyone could visualise easily, and imagine the amazing scene of the forest creatures resurrecting the totara tree. I like the idea of a powerful and watchful god image of Tane, so he is there as part of the forest, forming from the clouds." Nick would like to do a course in computer-aided design and aims to work in an area where he can utilise his artistic ability. He has already sold some of his own work to raise funds to represent New Zealand in basketball tournaments in Australia. Nick completed his illustration in Conneticut, USA, where he was accepted for a nine-month basketball scholarship.

**The Legend of Mauao** — *acrylic on cartridge*
Illustrated by Mark Hansen (16), Otumoetai College, Tauranga

"I wanted to portray the story with Maori figures throughout the border and include the night children, the clouds and the journey. For the image of the mountain I wanted it to be realistic, the way I've known it for 16 years, with a mysterious theme." Mark plans to take an art history or painting course in Wellington or Otago in 2000 and may study to be an art teacher, but would ultimately like to make a living from his art. He also plays rugby and is an alternative music fan.

**Pania of the Reef** — *oil on card*
Illustrated by Matt Wilmar (17), Kerikeri High School, Kerikeri

"I have been diving in the Bay of Islands so painting the underwater image is inspired by what I've seen first-hand. Art has always been very important to me and always will be. I can't remember a time when I didn't sketch or draw." Matt will continue to study painting and sculpture in the seventh form and plans to work in an art-related occupation after school. His other interests include soccer, surfing, volleyball and music.

**The Legend of Waikaremoana** — *acrylic on paper*
Illustrated by Shane Evans (17), Queen Charlotte College, Picton

Shane was born in Christchurch and his family belongs to the Ngai Tahu tribe. "I have liked drawing since I first started school and I taught myself how to draw." Shane plans to attend the Wellington Polytechnic School of Design and would like to become an architect or graphic designer.

**Maui and the Fingers of Fire** — *acrylic on card*
Illustrated by Debbie Milne (17), Cromwell College, Otago

"As I read the story I discovered a real sense of power within the character Mahuika. I wanted to show this by an incandescent glow which illuminates the rest of the page." Debbie hopes to pursue art at a tertiary level and gain a degree in Fine Arts majoring in painting. Living in Central Otago, she enjoys sports such as snowboarding and water activities on Lake Dunstan. She also plays an active role in school theatre productions.

**Hatupatu and the Bird Woman** — *acrylic on paper*
Illustrated by Martin Mihaka (15) and Reihana Pene (15), Western Heights High School, Rotorua

Martin is from the Te Arawa tribe. "All the boys in our family have been interested in art and I've always been interested in drawing." Martin intends continuing with art at tertiary level. His other interests include playing guitar, volleyball and computers.

Reihana is from the Te Arawa tribe. The influences for his painting come from his Maori background and his knowledge of the thermal environment of Rotorua. Reihana wants to take his art to the seventh form and have a career in the art field. "My father is a carver and my older brother was also very good at art at school." Reihana also enjoys volleyball, soccer, windsurfing, playing guitar and music.

**The Lone Fairy of Pirongia** — *acrylic and mixed media on paper*
Illustrated by Tukukino George (17), Ngaruawahia High School, Ngaruawahia

Tukukino's ancestry comes from the Ngati Mahuta and Ngati Koriki Tainui tribes. "I was inspired by the narrative from the story, *'bony hands tearing at the sturdy pole'*. The words 'bony' and 'tearing' impacted my imagination as a visual contrast between kinetic movement and the static 'sturdy pole'. My interest in art not only extends into the visual arts but also into philosophy and the function of art and artists in society." In 1999 Tukukino intends to study body and tattoo art in Australia and would like to set up his own tattoo studio.

**Maui and the Sun** — *paper and tissue collage*
Illustrated by (l-r): Junita Browman (16), Elisha Bunn (17) and Anita Best (16), Lincoln High School, Canterbury

"We wanted to illustrate the story with something that packed a bit of punch. Using paper as our medium, we aimed to create well-executed and accurate designs of koru to make up Maui and the blinding sun. With the wide range of papers available on the market today, we felt that the textures and style would be easy to work with and have a distinctly interesting effect."

In 1999, Junita will be doing UB design and photography and hopes to go to Canterbury University and pursue a career in graphic design. Elisha also plans to become a graphic designer. She has enjoyed making things from an early age and the introduction of computers into the artworld has bought a new perspective to design for her. Anita's uncle is an artist and was the first to show Anita how to draw when she was young. Now she is interested in commercial design and also hopes to study at Canterbury University or Wellington Polytech.

**The Kuia and her Faithful Dog** — *acrylic on paper*
Illustrated by Yi-Chang Lin (17), St Pauls College, Auckland

Taiwanese Yi-Chang developed several different compositions and was inspired by the book *Mataora* by Sandy Adsett and Cliff Whiting for his illustration of the kuia and her dog. As well as taking part in the seventh form art curriculum of painting, printmaking and photography, Yi-Chang likes to do Chinese painting and has done an animation course. Other hobbies include basketball, movies and music. He plans to go to Auckland University's Elam Art School.

**The Battle of the Mountains** — *acrylic on card*
Illustrated by Angus Kerr (18), Auckland Grammar, Auckland

"To me, the legend shows an understanding of the geological forces shaping the landscape. The Maori knew that long ago there was a period of intense volcanic activity. Coupled with this understanding is human drama which in turn boosts the mana of the local Maori and their mountains." In 1999 Angus hopes to continue his art at tertiary level.

# GLOSSARY

On request from the author, macrons are not used in the main text but have been included in the glossary to indicate correct pronounciation.

**GODS OF THE MĀORI**
**Haumia:** God of cultivation (things that grow beneath the ground)
**Papatūanuku (Papa):** the great Earth Mother
**Ranginui (Rangi):** the great Sky Father
**Ruamoko:** God of earthquakes
**Rongo:** God of cultivation (things that grow above the ground)
**Tānemahuta (Tāne):** the firstborn of Papa and Rangi; god of the forests
**Tangaroa:** God of the oceans
**Tawhirimatea:** God of the winds
**Tū Matauenga:** God of man and war

**MĀORI PLACE NAMES**
**Aotearoa:** The Land of the Long White Cloud; New Zealand
**The Great Ocean of Kiwa:** The Pacific Ocean
**Hawaiiki:** the land from whence the Maori people came, now supposedly beneath the Great Ocean of Kiwa
**Hautere:** (fast wind) the name of the forest south of Tauranga, near Oropi
**Matakana:** a long island to the north of Mount Maunganui
**Mauao:** (lit up by the first rays of the sun) mountain of Tauranga Moana
**Maunganui:** (big mountain) once known as Mauao; a mountain in Tauranga Moana, on the end of a long, sandy spit
**Pihanga:** a beautiful female mountain to the south of Lake Taupo
**Pirongia:** a mystical mountain of the Waikato area
**Taranaki:** a volcano near the west coast of the North Island; the people and region surrounding this mountain (also called Mount Egmont)
**Taupō-nui-a-Tia:** the cloak of Tia, a large lake in central North Island
**Tauranga Moana:** (harbour); resting place for canoes; a city in the Bay of Plenty
**Te Ika a Māui:** (the fish of Māui) the North Island of New Zealand
**Tongariro, Ruapehu, Ngauruhoe, Tauhara, Putauaki:** male mountains of the central plateau in the North Island
**Waikaremoana:** (sea of dashing waters) a lake south-east of Rotorua
**Waikato:** a large river in the North Island; the people and region surrounding this river
**Waimapu:** (sobbing waters) a pa beside the Waimapu River near Tauranga

**MĀORI PHRASES**
**Aue! E hika!:** Cry of dismay
**E noho ra:** Farewell (to those who are staying)
**E whaea, kei hea ra koe?:** Mother, where are you?
**Hei aha ai?:** Why not?
**Kahore he wai:** There is no water
**Kia ora:** To life! (a greeting)
**Tena koe:** Greetings (to one person)
**Te wahine koretake! Upoko-kohua!:** Useless woman! Go boil your head! (In Maori anything to do with the head is sacred; this is therefore a terrible insult)

## OTHER MĀORI NAMES AND WORDS

**harakeke:** flax

**Hinepukoherangi:** maiden of the mist

**hui:** a gathering of people for a set purpose

**kahikatea:** white pine tree

**kāhu:** hawk

**kaikōmako:** *Pennantia corymbosa* tree

**kākā:** New Zealand parrot

**karakia:** prayer; powerful words of the ancient ones, handed down through generations

**kererū:** wood pigeon, part of the staple diet of the early Maori

**kiwi:** wingless, nocturnal bird

**kōriro:** shrill call of a bird

**kōura:** freshwater crayfish

**kuia:** old woman, grandmother

**kūmara:** sweet potato

**Kurungaituku:** the dreaded bird woman

**mahoe:** whiteywood tree

**marae:** land in front of the wharenui (meeting house); this land was ruled by Tū Matauenga. When welcoming visitors to the marae, all speeches are held here; all words that are needed to be said are spoken here

**Māui-tiki-tiki-a-Taranga:** the full name of the demi god Maui meaning Maui-who-was-wrapped-in-Taranga's-topknot

**mere:** battle club made of wood or greenstone, often intricately carved

**miro:** the red fleshy berries of this tree provide food for the kereru, which in turn gives the bird a distinctive flavour

**mokopuna:** grandchild, grandchildren

**ngaio:** a small, brittle, shrub-like tree

**pā:** fortified village

**pate:** seven-finger tree

**patupaiarehe:** fair-skinned fairy folk who come out at night

**piopio:** New Zealand thrush

**pīpīwharauroa:** cuckoo

**pīwakawaka:** bird, commonly known as the fantail

**poi:** flax ball on a string; originally a weapon of war, when given to womenfolk it was transformed into an object of beauty; the balls are swung in intricate patterns, striking against hands and bodies in rhythmical fashion

**ponga:** tree fern

**pōtiki:** youngest child

**puhi:** a much courted young woman who is not betrothed

**pukatea:** New Zealand laurel

**rimu:** red pine

**rīwai:** potato

**ruru:** New Zealand owl or morepork

**Tama-nui-te-Ra:** The Great Sun

**taniwha:** huge scaled beings with magical powers, like dragons, that dwell in watery places, some benevolent, others malevolent

**tapu:** sacred

**Te Marama:** The moon

**Te Rā:** The sun

**tōtara:** a tree very suitable for carving

**tuakana:** firstborn, eldest

**tuatua:** a bivalve shellfish plentiful on the beaches of Aotearoa

**tui:** Parson bird

**uenuku:** rainbow

**upoko:** head

**waka:** canoe

**whare:** dwelling

**wharekai:** dining room

**wharenui:** meeting house